MEET TWITCH AND THRASH!

adapted by May Nakamura

Ready-to-Read

Simon Spotlight

New York   London   Toronto   Sydney   New Delhi

SIMON SPOTLIGHT

An imprint of Simon & Schuster Children's Publishing Division
1230 Avenue of the Americas, New York, New York 10020
This Simon Spotlight edition July 2023

For information about special discounts for bulk purchases, please contact Simon & Schuster Special Sales at 1-866-506-1949 or business@simonandschuster.com.
Manufactured in United States of America 0523 LAK
10 9 8 7 6 5 4 3 2 1
ISBN 978-1-6659-3467-1 (hc)
ISBN 978-1-6659-3466-4 (pbk)
ISBN 978-1-6659-3468-8 (ebook)

Robby and Mo Malto
are new to Witwicky,
a quiet town.

Robby and Mo moved from the city for their mom's new job.
She is a park ranger.

Their dad is a history teacher
who loves Transformers robots.
They can turn into different vehicles
or animals.

All Transformers robots are strong fighters.

Optimus Prime, Bumblebee, Megatron, and Elita-1 are some of the most powerful bots ever!

Robby wants to leave Witwitcky and move back to the city. "There is nothing here that is worth staying for," he grumbles.

Mo convinces her brother
to go exploring outside with her.
She is excited by all the trees
and open fields.

One day, Robby and Mo discover
a cave glowing with blue light.
Inside the cave,
they find a large stone
surrounded by a shimmering pool.

Robby and Mo touch the stone. . . .
Suddenly, a strange material
wraps onto their arms!

It covers their arms like sleeves.
"It won't come off!" Robby shouts.

Two large robots rise from the pool.
Their eyes glow with the same light as
Robby's and Mo's sleeves.
The robots are Terrans . . .
the first Transformers robots
to be born on Earth!

Even though they've never met,
Robby and Mo somehow
know the names of the robots.
"Twitch and Thrash," Mo says.

Robby, Mo, Twitch, and Thrash
can feel one another's feelings, too.
When Twitch and Thrash feel afraid,
Robby can feel their fear.

When Mo calms down,
Twitch and Thrash do too.
"How would you feel about having
a sleepover and becoming
best friends?" Mo asks.
Robby and Mo feel a warm "Yes!"

There is just one problem, though.
What if Mom and Dad
don't want to adopt
Twitch and Thrash?

Robby decides to
hide the Terrans for now.
After all, Twitch and Thrash
first need to learn how to be
Transformers robots.

Twitch learns how to convert into a drone. "Wow, you have a vehicle mode!" Robby says.

"I want to change into something!" Thrash says.

"You have to stare at something really hard to change into it," Twitch tells him.

Thrash goes to the town square
to stare at other vehicles . . .
but nothing happens.

"The right set of wheels is a
huge choice.
You'll know it when you find it,"
Mo says.

Meanwhile, a dangerous man
named Mandroid
learns about the Terrans.

Mandroid's body has both human
and robot parts.
He wants to take apart the Terrans
and add them to his body.
Then he can become
even more powerful!

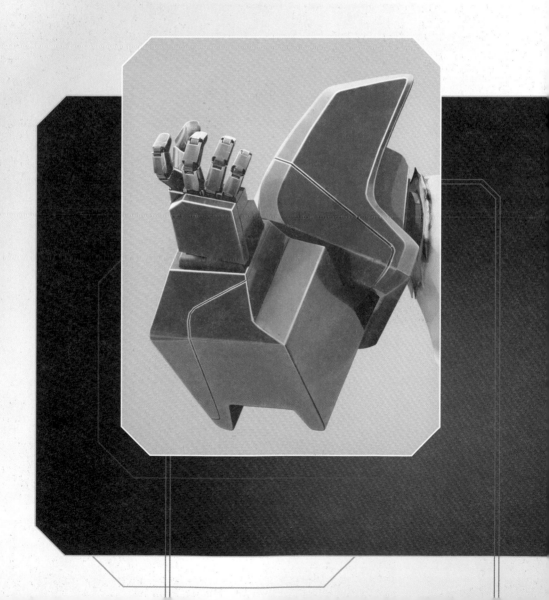

Mandroid kidnaps Twitch and Thrash. He traps them inside his lair.
"Tear them limb from limb!" he shouts.

Mandroid's spider robots
run toward the Terrans.
There are too many
for Twitch and Thrash
to fight on their own.

Then the Malto family arrives. They have come to save the day . . . with Optimus Prime, Megatron, Bumblebee, and Elita-1!

Twitch becomes a drone.
She flies, dodges, and attacks
in the air!

Then Thrash converts into a motorcycle. He zips, zooms, and outruns the enemy bots!

Mo jumps into Thrash's sidecar.
She is ready to ride!

Working as a team, they all escape
from Mandroid's lair.

"Twitch and Trash are bonded to Robby and Mo. That makes them family," Mom says.

The Maltos agree to adopt them.

"I think I like it here in Witwicky!"
Mo says.
"You know what?
I think I like it here too!"
Robby replies.